Taxi Dog

by Svend Otto

Parents' Magazine Press

New York

Translated from *Taxa-hunden Jesper,* published in Denmark by Gyldendalske
Boghandel 1977
Copyright © 1977 by Svend Otto S.
United States text adaptation copyright © 1978 by Parents' Magazine Press
Printed in the United States of America

10 9 8 7 6 5 4 3 2 1

Library of Congress Cataloging in Publication Data

Otto, Svend
  Taxi dog.
  Translation of Taxa-hunden Jesper.
  Summary: A taxi-riding mongrel with a zest for
life meets a very sweet dachshund.
  [1. Dogs—Fiction] I. Title.
PZ7.O893Tax   [E]   77-24127
ISBN 0-8193-0915-X
ISBN 0-8193-0916-8 lib. bdg.

Once upon a time, in Copenhagen, Denmark,
a small stray dog wandered up to a taxi stand.
The taxi drivers all liked him so much that
they gave him a name—Jasper—and bought him
a beautiful red collar.

The old grocer, whose shop was around the corner,
found him a basket to sleep in.
And he was given the job of rat catcher.

When the garbage men came early in the morning,

Jasper would wake up the grocer by scratching at his door.
Then Jasper was let out to catch rats. He was good at his job.

Afterwards, they walked to the bakery to buy bread for breakfast.

Jasper always got a pretzel as a reward.

He would carry it around the corner to the café,

where the waiter gave Jasper a large bowl of coffee
to go with his pretzel.

But, best of all, Jasper loved to ride in taxis.

Sometimes he took a taxi to a new part of the city,
and jumped off to explore.

When he was ready to move on, he caught another taxi.
Luckily, all taxicabs had running boards in those days.

In this way, Jasper traveled everywhere—
even far into the countryside.

One morning when the Royal Guards were on parade,

Jasper joined their march.

Another time he visited the railway station.

It was always easy finding a cab back to his own taxi stand.

Near the taxi stand there were some chickens.

One afternoon, as Jasper lay dozing,

a tire on his taxi blew out with an enormous BANG.

The chickens flew every which way in fright.

Jasper didn't know what to make of it all,
so he jumped over the fence and began chasing the chickens.

What a hullabaloo!

Maybe Jasper thought the chickens had caused the blowout.

In any case, the commotion brought a police officer.
"Come with me," he said,
and he rode off with Jasper trotting alongside.

As they passed the café,
a visiting farmer was sitting out front.
"Hmm. I could use a watchdog like that,"
he told the policeman.

And that was how Jasper was sent to the farm,

where he was tied up and kept in a doghouse.

How he missed all his friends in the city! So one morning
he gnawed through the rope and ran till he came to a road.

"I'll wait," he thought. "A taxi will come soon."

At last one came! It was an old bone-shaker,
but Jasper took it anyhow.

That evening Jasper was back at the grocer's door.
His old friend was glad to see him.

And Jasper might be taking taxis to this very day
if not for an accident. One morning,
as he was racing for a cab, Jasper was hit by a bus.

"He's done for this time," his friends thought sadly.

But, luckily for Jasper, they were wrong.
He was only stunned. Less than an hour later,
he was back home—

where he saw a charming dachshund.

She was, by far, the sweetest dog he had ever seen.

And Jasper forgot everything else—
the grocer,
the rats,
the pretzels,
the coffee at the café—
even riding around in taxis.
Imagine that!